'Desperate-minded villain!'

CHARLES DICKENS
Born 1812, Landport, England
Died 1870, Higham, England

Both stories taken from *Sketches by Boz*,
first published in 1839.

DICKENS IN PENGUIN CLASSICS
A Christmas Carol and Other Christmas Writings
A Tale of Two Cities
American Notes
Barnaby Rudge
Bleak House
David Copperfield
Dombey and Son
Great Expectations
Hard Times
Little Dorrit
Martin Chuzzlewit
Nicholas Nickleby
Oliver Twist
Our Mutual Friend
Pictures From Italy
Selected Journalism 1850–1870
Selected Short Fiction
Sketches by Boz
The Mystery of Edwin Drood
The Old Curiosity Shop
The Pickwick Papers

CHARLES DICKENS

The Great Winglebury Duel

PENGUIN BOOKS

PENGUIN CLASSICS

UK | USA | Canada | Ireland | Australia
India | New Zealand | South Africa

Penguin Books is part of the Penguin Random House group of companies
whose addresses can be found at global.penguinrandomhouse.com.

This selection published in Penguin Classics 2015
003

Set in 9/12.4 pt Baskerville 10 Pro
Typeset by Jouve (UK), Milton Keynes
Printed in Great Britain by Clays Ltd, St Ives plc

A CIP catalogue record for this book is available from the British Library

ISBN: 978-0-141-39715-3

www.greenpenguin.co.uk

Contents

The Great Winglebury Duel   1

The Steam Excursion   26

The Great Winglebury Duel

The little town of Great Winglebury is exactly forty-two miles and three-quarters from Hyde Park corner. It has a long, straggling, quiet High-street, with a great black and white clock at a small red Town-hall, half-way up – a market-place – a cage – an assembly-room – a church – a bridge – a chapel – a theatre – a library – an inn – a pump – and a Post-office. Tradition tells of a 'Little Winglebury' down some cross-road about two miles off; and as a square mass of dirty paper, supposed to have been originally intended for a letter, with certain tremulous characters inscribed thereon, in which a lively imagination might trace a remote resemblance to the word 'Little,' was once stuck up to be owned in the sunny window of the Great Winglebury Post-office, from which it only disappeared when it fell to pieces with dust and extreme old age, there would appear to be some foundation for the legend. Common belief is inclined to bestow the name upon a little hole at the end of a muddy lane about a couple of miles long, colonized by one wheelwright, four paupers, and a beer-shop; but even this authority, slight as it is, must be regarded with extreme suspicion, inasmuch as the inhabitants of the hole aforesaid concur in opining that it never had any name at all, from the earliest ages down to the present day.

The Winglebury Arms in the centre of the High-street,

opposite the small building with the big clock, is the principal inn of Great Winglebury – the commercial inn, posting-house, and excise-office; the 'Blue' house at every election, and the Judges' house at every assizes. It is the head-quarters of the Gentlemen's Whist Club of Winglebury Blues (so called in opposition to the Gentlemen's Whist Club of Winglebury Buffs, held at the other house, a little further down); and whenever a juggler, or wax-work man, or concert-giver, takes Great Winglebury in his circuit, it is immediately placarded all over the town that Mr So-and-so, 'trusting to that liberal support which the inhabitants of Great Winglebury have long been so liberal in bestowing, has at a great expense engaged the elegant and commodious assembly-rooms, attached to the Winglebury Arms.' The house is a large one, with a red brick and stone front; a pretty spacious hall ornamented with evergreen plants, terminates in a perspective view of the bar, and a glass case, in which are displayed a choice variety of delicacies ready for dressing, to catch the eye of a new-comer the moment he enters, and excite his appetite to the highest possible pitch. Opposite doors lead to the 'coffee' and 'commercial' rooms; and a great wide, rambling staircase, – three stairs and a landing – four stairs and another landing – one step and another landing – half a dozen stairs and another landing – and so on – conducts to galleries of bedrooms, and labyrinths of sitting-rooms, denominated 'private,' where you may enjoy yourself as privately as you can in any place where some bewildered being or other walks into your room every five minutes by mistake, and then walks out again, to open all the doors along the gallery till he finds his own.

Such is the Winglebury Arms at this day, and such was the Winglebury Arms some time since – no matter when – two or three minutes before the arrival of the London stage. Four horses with cloths on – change for a coach – were standing quietly at the corner of the yard, surrounded by a listless group of post-boys in shiny hats and smock-frocks, engaged in discussing the merits of the cattle; half a dozen ragged boys were standing a little apart, listening with evident interest to the conversation of these worthies; and a few loungers were collected round the horse-trough, awaiting the arrival of the coach.

The day was hot and sunny, the town in the zenith of its dulness, and with the exception of these few idlers, not a living creature was to be seen. Suddenly the loud notes of a key-bugle broke the monotonous stillness of the street; in came the coach, rattling over the uneven paving with a noise startling enough to stop even the large-faced clock itself. Down got the outsides, up went the windows in all directions; out came the waiters, up started the ostlers, and the loungers, and the post-boys, and the ragged boys, as if they were electrified – unstrapping, and unchaining, and unbuckling, and dragging willing horses out, and forcing reluctant horses in, and making a most exhilarating bustle. 'Lady inside, here,' said the guard. 'Please to alight, ma'am,' said the waiter. 'Private sitting-room?' interrogated the lady. – 'Certainly, ma'am,' responded the chambermaid. 'Nothing but these 'ere trunks, ma'am?' inquired the guard. 'Nothing more,' replied the lady. Up got the outsides again, and the guard, and the coachman; off came the cloths, with a jerk – 'All right' was the cry; and away they went. The loungers lingered a minute or two in the road, watching the coach till it turned the corner, and then loitered away one by one. The street was clear again, and the town, by contrast, quieter than ever.

'Lady in number twenty-five,' screamed the landlady. – 'Thomas!'

'Yes, ma'am.'

'Letter just been left for the gentleman in number nineteen. – Boots at the Lion left it. – No answer.'

'Letter for you, sir,' said Thomas, depositing the letter on number nineteen's table.

'For me?' said number nineteen, turning from the window, out of which he had been surveying the scene we have just described.

'Yes, sir, – (waiters always speak in hints, and never utter complete sentences) – yes, sir, – Boots at the Lion, sir – Bar, sir – Missis said number nineteen, sir – Alexander Trott, Esq., sir? – Your card at the bar, sir, I think, sir?'

'My name *is* Trott,' replied number nineteen, breaking the seal. 'You may go, waiter.' The waiter pulled down the window-blind, and then pulled it up again – for a regular waiter must do something before he leaves the room – adjusted the glasses on the sideboard, brushed a place which was *not* dusty, rubbed his hands very hard, walked stealthily to the door, and evaporated.

There was evidently something in the contents of the letter of a nature, if not wholly unexpected, certainly extremely disagreeable. Mr Alexander Trott laid it down and took it up again, and walked about the room on particular squares of the carpet, and even attempted, though very unsuccessfully, to whistle an air. It wouldn't do. He threw himself into a chair and read the following epistle aloud:

'Blue Lion and Stomach-warmer,
Great Winglebury.

'Wednesday Morning.

'SIR,

'Immediately on discovering your intentions, I left our counting-house, and followed you. I know the purport of your journey; – that journey shall never be completed.

'I have no friend here just now, on whose secrecy I can rely. This shall be no obstacle to my revenge. Neither shall Emily Brown be exposed to the mercenary solicitations of a scoundrel, odious in her eyes, and contemptible in every body else's: nor will I tamely submit to the clandestine attacks of a base umbrella-maker.

'Sir, – from Great Winglebury Church, a footpath leads through four meadows to a retired spot known to the townspeople as Stiffun's Acre (Mr Trott shuddered). I shall be waiting there alone, at twenty minutes before six o'clock to-morrow morning. Should I be disappointed of seeing you there, I will do myself the pleasure of calling with a horsewhip.

'HORACE HUNTER.

'PS. There is a gunsmith's in the High-street; and they won't sell gunpowder after dark – you understand me.

'PPS. You had better not order your breakfast in the morning till you have seen me. It may be an unnecessary expense.'

5

'Desperate-minded villain! I knew how it would be!' ejaculated the terrified Trott. 'I always told father, that once start me on this expedition, and Hunter would pursue me like the wandering Jew. It's bad enough as it is, to marry with the old people's commands, and without the girl's consent: but what will Emily think of me, if I go down there, breathless with running away from this infernal salamander? What *shall* I do? What *can* I do? If I go back to the city I'm disgraced for ever – lose the girl, and what's more lose the money too. Even if I did go on to the Brown's by the coach, Hunter would be after me in a post-chaise; and if I go to this place, this Stiffun's Acre, (another shudder) I'm as good as dead. I've seen him hit the man at the Pall-mall shooting gallery, in the second button-hole of the waistcoat five times out of every six, and when he didn't hit him there, he hit him in the head.' And with this consolatory reminiscence, Mr Alexander Trott again ejaculated, 'What shall I do?'

Long and weary were his reflections as, burying his face in his hands, he sat ruminating on the best course to be pursued. His mental direction-post pointed to London. He thought of 'the governor's' anger, and the loss of the fortune which the paternal Brown had promised the paternal Trott his daughter should contribute to the coffers of his son. Then the words 'To Brown's' were legibly inscribed on the said direction-post, but Horace Hunter's denunciation rung in his ears: – last of all it bore, in red letters, the words, 'To Stiffun's Acre;' and then Mr Alexander Trott decided on adopting a plan which he presently matured.

First and foremost he despatched the under-boots to the Blue Lion and Stomach-warmer, with a gentlemanly note to

Mr Horace Hunter, intimating that he thirsted for his destruction and would do himself the pleasure of slaughtering him next morning without fail. He then wrote another letter, and requested the attendance of the other boots – for they kept a pair. A modest knock at the room-door was heard – 'Come in,' said Mr Trott. A man thrust in a red head with one eye in it, and being again desired to 'come in,' brought in the body and legs to which the head belonged and a fur cap which belonged to the head.

'You are the upper-boots, I think?' inquired Mr Trott.

'Yes, I am the upper-boots,' replied a voice from inside a velveteen case with mother-of-pearl buttons – 'that is, I'm the boots as b'longs to the house; the other man's my man, as goes errands and does odd jobs – top-boots and half-boots I calls us.'

'You're from London?' inquired Mr Trott.

'Driv a cab once,' was the laconic reply.

'Why don't you drive it now?' asked Mr Trott.

'Cos I over-driv the cab, and driv over a 'ooman,' replied the top-boots, with brevity.

'Do you know the mayor's house?' inquired Trott.

'Rather,' replied the boots, significantly, as if he had some good reason to remember it.

'Do you think you could manage to leave a letter there?' interrogated Trott.

'Shouldn't wonder,' responded boots.

'But this letter,' said Trott, holding a deformed note with a paralytic direction in one hand, and five shillings in the other – 'this letter is anonymous.'

'A – what?' interrupted the boots.

7

'Anonymous – he's not to know who it comes from.'

'Oh! I see,' responded the rig'lar, with a knowing wink, but without evincing the slightest disinclination to undertake the charge – 'I see – bit o' sving, eh?' and his one eye wandered round the room as if in quest of a dark lantern and phosphorous-box. 'But I say,' he continued, recalling the eye from its search, and bringing it to bear on Mr Trott – 'I say, he's a lawyer, our mayor, and insured in the County. If you've a spite agen him, you'd better not burn his house down – blessed if I don't think it would be the greatest favour you could do him.' And he chuckled inwardly.

If Mr Alexander Trott had been in any other situation, his first act would have been to kick the man down stairs by deputy; or, in other words, to ring the bell, and desire the landlord to take his boots off. He contented himself, however, with doubling the fee and explaining that the letter merely related to a breach of the peace. The top-boots retired, solemnly pledged to secrecy; and Mr Alexander Trott sat down to a fried sole, maintenon cutlet, Madeira, and sundries, with much greater composure than he had experienced since the receipt of Horace Hunter's letter of defiance.

The lady who alighted from the London coach had no sooner been installed in number twenty-five, and made some alteration in her travelling-dress, than she endited a note to Joseph Overton, esquire, solicitor, and mayor of Great Winglebury, requesting his immediate attendance on private business of paramount importance – a summons which that worthy functionary lost no time in obeying; for after sundry openings of his eyes, divers ejaculations of 'Bless me!' and other manifestations of surprise, he took his broad-brimmed hat from its accustomed peg in his little front office, and walked briskly down the High-street to the Winglebury Arms; through the hall and up the staircase of which establishment he was ushered by the landlady, and a crowd of officious waiters, to the door of number twenty-five.

'Show the gentleman in,' said the stranger lady, in reply to the foremost waiter's announcement. The gentleman was shown in accordingly.

The lady rose from the sofa; the mayor advanced a step from the door, and there they both paused for a minute or two, looking at one another as if by mutual consent. The mayor saw before him a buxom richly-dressed female of about forty; and the lady looked upon a sleek man about ten years older, in drab shorts and continuations, black coat, neckcloth, and gloves.

'Miss Julia Manners!' exclaimed the mayor at length, 'you astonish me.'

'That's very unfair of you, Overton,' replied Miss Julia, 'for I have known you long enough not to be surprised at any thing you do, and you might extend equal courtesy to me.'

'But to run away – actually run away – with a young man!' remonstrated the mayor.

'You would not have me actually run away with an old one I presume?' was the cool rejoinder.

'And then to ask me – me – of all people in the world – a man of my age and appearance – mayor of the town – to promote such a scheme!' pettishly ejaculated Joseph Overton; throwing himself into an arm-chair, and producing Miss

9

Julia's letter from his pocket, as if to corroborate the assertion that he had been asked.

'Now, Overton,' replied the lady, impatiently, 'I want your assistance in this matter, and I must have it. In the lifetime of that poor old dear, Mr Cornberry, who – who –'

'Who was to have married you, and didn't because he died first; and who left you his property unencumbered with the addition of himself,' suggested the mayor, in a sarcastic tone.

'Well,' replied Miss Julia, reddening slightly, 'in the lifetime of the poor old dear, the property had the incumbrance of your management; and all I will say of that is, that I only wonder *it* didn't die of consumption instead of its master. You helped yourself then: – help me now.'

Mr Joseph Overton was a man of the world, and an attorney; and as certain indistinct recollections of an odd thousand pounds or two, appropriated by mistake, passed across his mind, he hemmed deprecatingly, smiled blandly, remained silent for a few seconds; and finally inquired, 'What do you wish me to do?'

'I'll tell you,' replied Miss Julia – 'I'll tell you in three words. Dear Lord Peter –'

'That's the young man, I suppose –' interrupted the mayor.

'That's the young nobleman,' replied the lady, with a great stress on the last word. 'Dear Lord Peter is considerably afraid of the resentment of his family; and we have therefore thought it better to make the match a stolen one. He left town to avoid suspicion, on a visit to his friend, the Honourable Augustus Flair, whose seat, as you know, is about thirty miles from this, accompanied only by his favourite tiger. We arranged that I should come here alone in the

London coach; and that he, leaving his tiger and cab behind him, should come on, and arrive here as soon as possible this afternoon.'

'Very well,' observed Joseph Overton, 'and then he can order the chaise, and you can go on to Gretna Green together, without requiring the presence or interference of a third party, can't you?'

'No,' replied Miss Julia. 'We have every reason to believe – dear Lord Peter not being considered very prudent or sagacious by his friends, and they having discovered his attachment to me – that immediately on his absence being observed, pursuit will be made in this direction: to elude which, and to prevent our being traced, I wish it to be understood in this house, that dear Lord Peter is slightly deranged, though perfectly harmless; and that I am, unknown to him, waiting his arrival to convey him in a post-chaise to a private asylum – at Berwick, say. If I don't show myself much, I dare say I can manage to pass for his mother.'

The thought occurred to the mayor's mind that the lady might show herself a good deal without fear of detection; seeing that she was about double the age of her intended husband. He said nothing, however, and the lady proceeded –

'With the whole of this arrangement, dear Lord Peter is acquainted: and all I want you to do is, to make the delusion more complete by giving it the sanction of your influence in this place, and assigning this as a reason to the people of the house for my taking the young gentleman away. As it would not be consistent with the story that I should see him until after he has entered the chaise, I also wish you to communicate with him, and inform him that it is all going on well.'

'Has he arrived?' inquired Overton.

'I don't know,' replied the lady.

'Then how am I to know?' inquired the mayor. 'Of course he will not give his own name at the bar.'

'I begged him, immediately on his arrival, to write you a note,' replied Miss Manners; 'and to prevent the possibility of our project being discovered through its means, I desired him to write anonymously, and in mysterious terms to acquaint you with the number of his room.'

'God bless me!' exclaimed the mayor, rising from his seat, and searching his pockets – 'most extraordinary circumstance – he *has* arrived – mysterious note left at my house in a most mysterious manner, just before yours – didn't know what to make of it before, and certainly shouldn't have attended to it. – Oh! here it is.' And Joseph Overton pulled out of an inner coat-pocket the identical letter penned by Alexander Trott. 'Is this his lordship's hand?'

'Oh yes,' replied Julia; 'good, punctual creature! I have not seen it more than once or twice, but I know he writes very badly and very large. These dear, wild young noblemen, you know, Overton –'

'Ay, ay, I see,' replied the mayor. – 'Horses and dogs, play and wine – grooms, actresses, and cigars, – the stable, the green-room, the brothel, and the tavern; and the legislative assembly at last.'

'Here's what he says,' pursued the mayor; '"Sir, – A young gentleman in number nineteen at the Winglebury Arms, is bent on committing a rash act to-morrow morning at an early hour. (That's good – he means marrying.) If you have any regard for the peace of this town, or the preservation of one – it may be two – human lives" – What the deuce does he mean by that?'

'That he's so anxious for the ceremony, he will expire if it's put off, and that I may possibly do the same,' replied the lady with great complacency.

'Oh! I see – not much fear of that; – well – "two human lives, you will cause him to be removed to-night. – (He wants to start at once.) Fear not to do this on your responsibility: for to-morrow, the absolute necessity of the proceeding will be but too aparent. Remember: number nineteen. The name is Trott. No delay; for life and death depend upon your promptitude." – Passionate language, certainly. – Shall I see him?'

'Do,' replied Miss Julia; 'and entreat him to act his part well. I am half afraid of him. Tell him to be cautious.'

'I will,' said the mayor.

'Settle all the arrangements.'

'I will,' said the mayor again.

'And say I think the chaise had better be ordered for one o'clock.'

'Very well,' cried the mayor once more; and ruminating on the absurdity of the situation in which fate and old acquaintance had placed him, he desired a waiter to herald his approach to the temporary representative of number nineteen.

The announcement – 'Gentleman to speak with you, sir,' induced Mr Trott to pause half-way in the glass of port, the contents of which he was in the act of imbibing at the moment; to rise from his chair, and retreat a few paces towards the window, as if to secure a retreat in the event of the visitor assuming the form and appearance of Horace Hunter. One glance at Joseph Overton, however, quieted his apprehensions. He courteously motioned the stranger to a seat. The waiter after a little jingling with the decanter and glasses, consented to leave the room; and Joseph Overton placing the broad-brimmed hat on the chair next him, and bending his body gently forward, opened the business by saying in a very low and cautious tone,

'My lord –'

'Eh?' said Mr Alexander Trott in a very loud key, with the vacant and mystified stare of a chilly somnambulist.

'Hush – hush!' said the cautious attorney: 'to be sure – quite right – no titles here – my name is Overton, sir.'

'Overton!'

'Yes: the mayor of this place – you sent me a letter with anonymous information, this afternoon.'

'I, sir?' exclaimed Trott with ill-dissembled surprise; for, coward as he was, he would willingly have repudiated the authorship of the letter in question. 'I, sir?'

'Yes, you, sir; did you not?' responded Overton, annoyed with what he supposed to be an extreme degree of unnecessary suspicion. 'Either this letter is yours, or it is not. If it be, we can converse securely upon the subject at once. If it be not, of course I have no more to say.'

'Stay, stay,' said Trott, 'it *is* mine; I *did* write it. What could I do, sir? I had no friend here.'

'To be sure – to be sure,' said the mayor, encouragingly, 'you could not have managed it better. Well, sir; it will be necessary for you to leave here to-night in a post-chaise and four. And the harder the boys drive the better. You are not safe from pursuit here.'

'Bless me!' exclaimed Trott, in an agony of apprehension, 'can such things happen in a country like this? Such unrelenting and cold-blooded hostility!' He wiped off the concentrated essence of cowardice that was oozing fast down his forehead, and looked aghast at Joseph Overton.

'It certainly is a very hard case,' replied the mayor with a smile, 'that, in a free country, people can't marry whom they like without being hunted down as if they were criminals. However, in the present instance the lady is willing, you know, and that's the main point, after all.'

'Lady willing!' repeated Trott, mechanically – 'How do you know the lady's willing?'

'Come, that's a good one,' said the mayor, benevolently tapping Mr Trott on the arm with his broad-brimmed hat, 'I have known her, well, for a long time, and if any body could entertain the remotest doubt on the subject, I assure you I have none, nor need you.'

'Dear me!' said Mr Trott, ruminating – 'Dear me! – this is very extraordinary!'

'Well, Lord Peter,' said the mayor, rising.

'Lord Peter?' repeated Mr Trott.

'Oh – ah, I forgot; well, Mr Trott, then – Trott – very good, ha! ha! – Well, sir, the chaise shall be ready at half-past twelve.'

'And what is to become of me till then?' inquired Mr Trott, anxiously. 'Wouldn't it save appearances if I were placed under some restraint?'

'Ah!' replied Overton, 'very good thought – capital idea indeed. I'll send somebody up directly. And if you make a little resistance when we put you in the chaise it wouldn't be amiss – look as if you didn't want to be taken away, you know.'

'To be sure,' said Trott – 'to be sure.'

'Well, my lord,' said Overton, in a low tone, 'till then, I wish your lordship a good evening.'

'Lord – lordship!' ejaculated Trott again, falling back a step or two, and gazing in unutterable wonder on the countenance of the mayor.

'Ha-ha! I see, my lord – practising the madman? – very good indeed – very vacant look – capital, my lord, capital – good evening, Mr Trott – ha! ha! ha!'

'That mayor's decidedly drunk,' soliloquised Mr Trott, throwing himself back in his chair, in an attitude of reflection.

'He is a much cleverer fellow than I thought him, that young nobleman – he carries it off uncommonly well,' thought Overton, as he wended his way to the bar, there to complete his arrangements. This was soon done: every word of the story was implicitly believed, and the one-eyed boots was immediately instructed to repair to number nineteen, to act as custodian of the person of the supposed lunatic until half-past twelve o'clock. In pursuance of this direction, that somewhat eccentric gentleman armed himself with a walking-stick of gigantic dimensions, and repaired with his usual equanimity of manner to Mr Trott's apartment, which he entered without any ceremony, and mounted guard in, by quietly depositing himself upon a chair near the door, where he proceeded to beguile the time by whistling a popular air with great apparent satisfaction.

'What do you want here, you scoundrel?' exclaimed Mr Alexander Trott, with a proper appearance of indignation at his detention.

The boots beat time with his head, as he looked gently round at Mr Trott with a smile of pity, and whistled an *adagio* movement.

'Do you attend in this room by Mr Overton's desire?' inquired Trott, rather astonished at the man's demeanour.

'Keep yourself to yourself, young feller,' calmly responded the boots, 'and don't say nothin' to nobody.' And he whistled again.

'Now mind,' ejaculated Mr Trott, anxious to keep up the farce of wishing with great earnestness to fight a duel if they'd let him, – 'I protest against being kept here. I deny that I have any intention of fighting with any body. But as it's useless contending with superior numbers, I shall sit quietly down.'

'You'd better,' observed the placid boots, shaking the large stick expressively.

'Under protest, however,' added Alexander Trott, seating himself, with indignation in his face but great content in his heart. 'Under protest.'

'Oh, certainly!' responded the boots; 'any thing you please. If you're happy, I'm transported; only don't talk too much – it'll make you worse.'

'Make me worse!' exclaimed Trott, in unfeigned astonishment: 'the man's drunk!'

George Cruikshank

'You'd better be quiet, young feller,' remarked the boots, going through a most threatening piece of pantomime with the stick.

'Or mad!' said Mr Trott, rather alarmed. 'Leave the room, sir, and tell them to send somebody else.'

'Won't do!' replied the boots.

'Leave the room!' shouted Trott, ringing the bell violently; for he began to be alarmed on a new score.

'Leave that 'ere bell alone, you wretched loo-nattic!' said the boots, suddenly forcing the unfortunate Trott back into his chair, and brandishing the stick aloft. 'Be quiet, you mis'rable object, and don't let every body know there's a madman in the house.'

'He *is* a madman! He *is* a madman!' exclaimed the terrified Mr Trott, gazing on the one eye of the red-headed boots with a look of abject horror.

'Madman!' replied the boots – 'dam'me, I think he *is* a madman with a vengeance! Listen to me, you unfort'nate. Ah! would you? – [a slight tap on the head with the large stick, as Mr Trott made another move towards the bell-handle] I caught you there! did I?'

'Spare my life!' exclaimed Trott, raising his hands imploringly.

'I don't want your life,' replied the boots, disdainfully, 'though I think it 'ud be a charity if somebody took it.'

'No, no, it wouldn't,' interrupted poor Mr Trott, hurriedly; 'no, no, it wouldn't! I – I –'d rather keep it!'

'O werry well,' said the boots; 'that's a mere matter of taste – ev'ry one to his liking. Hows'ever, all I've got to say is this here: You sit quietly down in that chair, and I'll sit

19

hoppersite you here, and if you keep quiet and don't stir, I won't damage you; but if you move hand or foot till half-past twelve o'clock, I shall alter the expression of your countenance so completely, that the next time you look in the glass you'll ask vether you're gone out of town, and ven you're likely to come back again. So sit down.'

'I will – I will,' responded the victim of mistakes; and down sat Mr Trott and down sat the boots too, exactly opposite him, with the stick ready for immediate action in case of emergency.

Long and dreary were the hours that followed. The bell of Great Winglebury church had just struck ten, and two hours and a half would probably elapse before succour arrived. For half an hour the noise occasioned by shutting up the shops in the street beneath betokened something like life in the town, and rendered Mr Trott's situation a little less insupportable; but when even these ceased, and nothing was heard beyond the occasional rattling of a post-chaise as it drove up the yard to change horses, and then drove away again, or the clattering of horses' hoofs in the stables behind, it became almost unbearable. The boots occasionally moved an inch or two, to knock superfluous bits of wax off the candles, which were burning low, but instantaneously resumed his former position; and as he remembered to have heard somewhere or other that the human eye had an unfailing effect in controlling mad people, he kept his solitary organ of vision constantly fixed on Mr Alexander Trott. That unfortunate individual stared at his companion in his turn, until his features grew more and more indistinct – his hair gradually less red – and the room more misty and obscure.

Mr Alexander Trott fell into a sound sleep, from which he was awakened by a rumbling in the street, and a cry of – 'Chaise-and-four for number twenty-five!' A bustle on the stairs succeeded; the room-door was hastily thrown open; and Mr Joseph Overton entered, followed by four stout waiters, and Mrs Williamson, the stout landlady of the Winglebury Arms.

'Mr Overton!' exclaimed Mr Alexander Trott, jumping up in a frenzy of passionate excitement – 'Look at this man, sir; consider the situation in which I have been placed for three hours past – the person you sent to guard me, sir, was a madman – a madman – a raging, ravaging, furious madman.'

'Bravo!' whispered Overton.

'Poor dear!' said the compassionate Mrs Williamson, 'mad people always thinks other people's mad.'

'Poor dear!' ejaculated Mr Alexander Trott, 'What the devil do you mean by poor dear! are you the landlady of this house?'

'Yes, yes,' replied the stout old lady, 'don't exert yourself, there's a dear – consider your health, now; do.'

'Exert myself!' shouted Mr Alexander Trott, 'it's a mercy, ma'am, that I have any breath to exert myself with, I might have been assassinated three hours ago by that one-eyed monster with the oakum head. How dare you have a madman, ma'am – how dare you have a madman, to assault and terrify the visiters to your house?'

'I'll never have another,' said Mrs Williamson, casting a look of reproach at the mayor.

'Capital – capital,' whispered Overton again, as he enveloped Mr Alexander Trott in a thick travelling-cloak.

'Capital, sir!' exclaimed Trott, aloud, 'it's horrible. The very recollection makes me shudder. I'd rather fight four duels in three hours if I survived the first three, than I'd sit for that time face to face with a madman.'

'Keep it up, as you go down stairs,' whispered Overton, 'your bill is paid, and your portmanteau in the chaise.' And then he added aloud, 'Now, waiters, the gentleman's ready.'

At this signal the waiters crowded round Mr Alexander Trott. One took one arm, another the other, a third walked before with a candle, the fourth behind with another candle; the boots and Mrs Williamson brought up the rear, and down stairs they went, Mr Alexander Trott expressing alternately at the very top of his voice either his feigned reluctance to go, or his unfeigned indignation at being shut up with a madman.

Mr Overton was waiting at the chaise-door, the boys were ready mounted, and a few ostlers and stable nondescripts were standing round to witness the departure of 'the mad gentleman.' Mr Alexander Trott's foot was on the step, when he observed (which the dim light had prevented his doing before) a human figure seated in the chaise, closely muffled up in a cloak like his own.

'Who's that?' he inquired of Overton, in a whisper.

'Hush, hush,' replied the mayor; 'the other party of course.'

'The other party!' exclaimed Trott, with an effort to retreat.

'Yes, yes; you'll soon find that out, before you go far, I should think – but make a noise, you'll excite suspicion if you whisper to me so much.'

'I won't go in this chaise,' shouted Mr Alexander Trott, all his original fears recurring with tenfold violence. 'I shall be assassinated – I shall be –'

'Bravo, bravo,' whispered Overton. 'I'll push you in.'

'But I won't go,' exclaimed Mr Trott. 'Help here, help! they're carrying me away against my will. This is a plot to murder me.'

'Poor dear!' said Mrs Williamson again.

'Now, boys, put 'em along,' cried the mayor, pushing Trott in and slamming the door. 'Off with you as quick as you can, and stop for nothing till you come to the next stage – all right.'

'Horses are paid, Tom,' screamed Mrs Williamson; and away went the chaise at the rate of fourteen miles an hour, with Mr Alexander Trott and Miss Julia Manners carefully shut up in the inside.

Mr Alexander Trott remained coiled up in one corner of the chaise, and his mysterious companion in the other, for the first two or three miles; Mr Trott edging more and more into his corner as he felt his companion gradually edging more and more from hers; and vainly endeavouring in the darkness to catch a glimpse of the furious face of the supposed Horace Hunter.

'We may speak now,' said his fellow traveller, at length; 'the post-boys can neither see nor hear us.'

'That's not Hunter's voice!' – thought Alexander, astonished.

'Dear Lord Peter!' said Miss Julia, most winningly: putting her arm on Mr Trott's shoulder – 'Dear Lord Peter. Not a word?'

'Why, it's a woman!' exclaimed Mr Trott in a low tone of excessive wonder.

'Ah – whose voice is that?' said Julia – ''tis not Lord Peter's.'

'No, – it's mine,' replied Mr Trott.

'Yours!' ejaculated Miss Julia Manners, 'a strange man! Gracious Heaven – how came you here?'

'Whoever you are, you might have known that I came against my will, ma'am,' replied Alexander, 'For I made noise enough when I got in.'

'Do you come from Lord Peter?' inquired Miss Manners.

'Damn Lord Peter,' replied Trott pettishly – 'I don't know any Lord Peter – I never heard of him before to-night, when I've been Lord Peter'd by one and Lord Peter'd by another, till I verily believe I'm mad, or dreaming –'

'Whither are we going?' inquired the lady tragically.

'How should *I* know, ma'am?' replied Trott with singular coolness; for the events of the evening had completely hardened him.

'Stop! stop!' cried the lady, letting down the front glasses of the chaise.

'Stay, my dear ma'am!' said Mr Trott, pulling the glasses up again with one hand, and gently squeezing Miss Julia's waist with the other. 'There is some mistake here; give me till the end of this stage to explain my share of it. We must go so far; you cannot be set down here alone, at this hour of the night.'

The lady consented; the mistake was mutually explained. Mr Trott was a young man, had highly promising whiskers, an undeniable tailor, and an insinuating address – he wanted nothing but valour, and who wants that with three thousand a-year? The lady had this, and more; she wanted a young husband, and the only course open to Mr Trott to retrieve his disgrace was a rich wife. So, they came to the conclusion that it would be a pity to have all this trouble and expense for nothing, and that as they were so far on the road already, they had better go to Gretna Green, and marry each other, and they did so. And the very next preceding entry in the Blacksmith's book was an entry of the marriage of Emily Brown with Horace Hunter. Mr Hunter took his wife home, and begged pardon, and *was* pardoned; and Mr Trott took *his* wife home, begged pardon too, and was pardoned also. And Lord Peter, who had been detained beyond his time by drinking champagne and riding a steeple-chase, went back to the Honourable Augustus Flair's, and drank more champagne, and rode another steeple-chase, and was thrown and killed. And Horace Hunter took great credit to himself for practising on the cowardice of Alexander Trott; and all these circumstances were discovered in time, and carefully noted down; and if ever you stop a week at the Winglebury Arms, they'll give you just this account of The Great Winglebury Duel.

The Steam Excursion

Mr Percy Noakes was a law-student, inhabiting a set of chambers on the fourth floor, in one of those houses in Gray's-inn-square which command an extensive view of the gardens, and their usual adjuncts – flaunting nursery-maids, and town-made children, with parenthetical legs. Mr Percy Noakes was what is generally termed – 'a devilish good fellow.' He had a large circle of acquaintance, and seldom dined at his own expense. He used to talk politics to papas, flatter the vanity of mammas, do the amiable to their daughters, make pleasure engagements with their sons, and romp with the younger branches. Like those paragons of perfection, advertising footmen out of place, he was always 'willing to make himself generally useful.' If any old lady, whose son was in India, gave a ball, Mr Percy Noakes was master of the ceremonies; if any young lady made a stolen match, Mr Percy Noakes gave her away; if a juvenile wife presented her husband with a blooming cherub, Mr Percy Noakes was either godfather, or deputy-godfather; and if any member of a friend's family died, Mr Percy Noakes was invariably to be seen in the second mourning coach, with a white handkerchief to his eyes, sobbing – to use his own appropriate and expressive description – 'like winkin!'

It may readily be imagined that these numerous avocations were rather calculated to interfere with Mr Percy

Noakes's professional studies. Mr Percy Noakes was perfectly aware of the fact, and he had, therefore, after mature reflection, made up his mind not to study at all – a laudable determination, to which he adhered in the most praiseworthy manner. His sitting-room presented a strange chaos of dress-gloves, boxing-gloves, caricatures, albums, invitation-cards, foils, cricket-bats, card-board drawings, paste, gum, and fifty other extraordinary articles heaped together in the strangest confusion. He was always making something for somebody, or planning some party of pleasure, which was his great *forte*. He invariably spoke with astonishing rapidity; was smart, spoffish, and eight-and-twenty.

'Splendid idea, 'pon my life!' soliloquized Mr Percy Noakes, over his morning's coffee, as his mind reverted to a suggestion which had been thrown out the previous night, by a lady at whose house he had spent the evening. 'Glorious idea! – Mrs Stubbs,' cried the student, raising his voice.

'Yes, sir,' replied a dirty old woman with an inflamed countenance, emerging from the bedroom, with a barrel of dirt and cinders. – This was the laundress. 'Did you call, sir?'

'Oh! Mrs Stubbs, I'm going out: if that tailor should call again, you'd better say – you'd better say, I'm out of town, and shan't be back for a fortnight; and if that bootmaker should come, tell him I've lost his address, or I'd have sent him that little amount. Mind he writes it down; and if Mr Hardy should call – you know Mr Hardy?'

'The funny gentleman, sir?'

'Ah! the funny gentleman. If Mr Hardy should call, say I've gone to Mrs Taunton's about that water-party.'

'Yes, sir.'

'And if any fellow calls, and says he's come about a steamer, tell him to be here at five o'clock this afternoon, Mrs Stubbs.'

'Very well, sir.'

Mr Percy Noakes brushed his hat, whisked the crumbs off his inexplicables with a silk handkerchief, gave the ends of his hair a persuasive roll round his forefinger, and sallied forth for Mrs Taunton's domicile in Great Marlborough-street, where she and her daughters occupied the upper part of a house. She was a good-looking widow of fifty, with the form of a giantess and the mind of a child. The pursuit of pleasure, and some means of killing time, appeared the sole end of her existence. She doted on her daughters, who were as frivolous as herself.

A general exclamation of satisfaction hailed the arrival of Mr Percy Noakes, who went through the ordinary salutations and threw himself into an easy chair near the ladies' work-table, with all the ease of a regularly established friend of the family. Mrs Taunton was busily engaged in planting immense bright bows on every part of a smart cap on which it was possible to stick one; Miss Emily Taunton was making a watch-guard; and Miss Sophia was at the piano, practising a new song – poetry by the young officer, or the police officer, or the custom-house officer, or some equally interesting amateur.

'You good creature!' said Mrs Taunton, addressing the gallant Percy. 'You really are a good soul! You've come about the water-party, I know.'

'I should rather suspect I had,' replied Mr Noakes, triumphantly. 'Now come here, girls, and I'll tell you all about it.' Miss Emily and Miss Sophia advanced to the table, with that ballet sort of step which some young ladies seem to think so fascinating – something between a skip and a canter.

'Now,' continued Mr Percy Noakes, 'it seems to me that the best way will be to have a committee of ten, to make all the arrangements, and manage the whole set-out. Then I propose that the expenses shall be paid by these ten fellows jointly.'

'Excellent, indeed!' said Mrs Taunton, who highly approved of this part of the arrangements.

'Then my plan is, that each of these ten fellows shall have the power of asking five people. There must be a meeting of the committee at my chambers, to make all the arrangements, and these people shall be then named; every member of the committee shall have the power of black-balling any one who is proposed, and one black ball shall exclude that person. This will ensure our having a pleasant party, you know.'

'What a manager you are!' interrupted Mrs Taunton again.

'Charming!' said the lovely Emily.

'I never did!' ejaculated Sophia.

'Yes, I think it'll do,' replied Mr Percy Noakes, who was now quite in his element. 'I think it'll do. Then you know we shall go down to the Nore and back, and have a regular capital cold dinner laid out in the cabin before we start, so that every thing may be ready without any confusion; and we shall have the lunch laid out on deck in those little tea-garden-looking concerns by the paddle-boxes – I don't know what you call 'em. Then we shall hire a steamer expressly for our party, and a band, and have the deck chalked, and we shall be able to dance quadrilles all day: and then whoever we know that's musical, you know, why they'll make themselves useful and agreeable; and – and – upon the whole, I really hope we shall have a glorious day, you know.'

The announcement of these arrangements was received with the utmost enthusiasm. Mrs Taunton, Emily, and Sophia, were loud in their praises.

'Well, but tell me, Percy,' said Mrs Taunton, 'who are the ten gentlemen to be?'

'Oh! I know plenty of fellows who'll be delighted with the scheme,' replied Mr Percy Noakes; 'of course, we shall have —'

'Mr Hardy,' interrupted the servant, announcing a visitor. Miss Sophia and Miss Emily hastily assumed the most interesting attitudes that could be adopted on so short a notice.

'How are you?' said a stout gentleman of about forty, pausing at the door in the attitude of an awkward harlequin. This was Mr Hardy, whom we have before described, on the authority of Mrs Stubbs, as 'the funny gentleman.' He was an Astley-Cooperish Joe Miller – a practical joker, immensely popular with married ladies, and a general favourite with young men. He was always engaged in some pleasure excursion or other, and delighted in getting somebody into a scrape on such occasions. He could sing comic songs, imitate hackney-coachmen and fowls, play airs on his chin, and execute concertos on the Jews'-harp. He always eat and drank most immoderately, and was the bosom friend of Mr Percy Noakes. He had a red face, a somewhat husky voice, and a tremendously loud laugh.

'How are you?' said this worthy, laughing, as if it were the finest joke in the world to make a morning call, and shaking hands with the ladies with as much vehemence as if their arms were so many pump-handles.

'You're just the very man I wanted,' said Mr Percy Noakes,

who proceeded to explain the cause of his being in requisition.

'Ha! ha! ha!' shouted Hardy, after hearing the statement, and receiving a detailed account of the proposed excursion. 'Oh, capital! glorious! What a day it will be! what fun! – But, I say, when are you going to begin making the arrangements?'

'No time like the present – at once, if you please.'

'Oh, charming!' cried the ladies. 'Pray, do.'

Writing materials were laid before Mr Percy Noakes, and the names of the different members of the committee were agreed on, after as much discussion between him and Mr Hardy as if at least the fate of nations had depended on their appointment. It was then agreed that a meeting should take place at Mr Percy Noakes's chambers on the ensuing Wednesday evening at eight o'clock, and the visiters departed.

Wednesday evening arrived, eight o'clock came, and eight members of the committee were punctual in their attendance. Mr Loggins, the solicitor, of Boswell-court, sent an excuse, and Mr Samuel Briggs, the ditto of Furnival's Inn, sent his brother, much to his (the brother's) satisfaction, and greatly to the discomfiture of Mr Percy Noakes. Between the Briggses and the Tauntons there existed a degree of implacable hatred, quite unprecedented. The animosity between the Montagues and Capulets was nothing to that which prevailed between these two illustrious houses. Mrs Briggs was a widow, with three daughters and two sons; Mr Samuel, the eldest, was an attorney, and Mr Alexander, the youngest, was under articles to his brother. They resided in Portland-street, Oxford-street, and moved in the same orbit as the

Tauntons – hence their mutual dislike. If the Miss Briggs appeared in smart bonnets, the Miss Tauntons eclipsed them with smarter. If Mrs Taunton appeared in a cap of all the hues of the rainbow, Mrs Briggs forthwith mounted a toque, with all the patterns of a kaleidescope. If Miss Sophia Taunton learnt a new song, two of the Miss Briggses came out with a new duet. The Tauntons had once gained a temporary triumph with the assistance of a harp, but the Briggses brought three guitars into the field, and effectually routed the enemy. There was no end to the rivalry between them.

Now, as Mr Samuel Briggs was a mere machine, a sort of self-acting legal walking-stick; and as the party was known to have originated, however remotely, with Mrs Taunton, the female branches of the Briggs family had arranged that Mr Alexander should attend instead of his brother; and as the said Mr Alexander was deservedly celebrated for possessing all the pertinacity of a bankruptcy-court attorney, combined with the obstinacy of that pleasing animal which browses upon the thistle – he required but little tuition. He was especially enjoined to make himself as disagreeable as possible; and, above all, to black-ball the Tauntons at every hazard.

The proceedings of the evening were opened by Mr Percy Noakes. After successfully urging upon the gentlemen present the propriety of their mixing some brandy-and-water, he briefly stated the object of the meeting, and concluded by observing that the first step must be the selection of a chairman, necessarily possessing some arbitrary – he trusted not unconstitutional – powers, to whom the personal direction of the whole of the arrangements (subject to the approval of the committee) should be confided. A pale young gentleman in a green stock and spectacles of the same, a member of the honourable society of the Inner Temple, immediately rose for the purpose of proposing Mr Percy Noakes. He had known him long, and this he would say, that a more honourable, a more excellent, or a better-hearted fellow, never existed – (hear, hear!) The young gentleman, who was a member of a debating society, took this opportunity of entering into an examination of the state of the English law, from the days of William the Conqueror down to the present period: he briefly adverted to the code established by the ancient Druids; slightly glanced at the principles laid down by the Athenian lawgivers; and concluded with a most glowing eulogium on pic-nics and constitutional rights.

Mr Alexander Briggs opposed the motion. He had the highest esteem for Mr Percy Noakes as an individual, but he did consider that he ought not to be intrusted with these immense powers – (oh, oh!) – He believed that in the proposed capacity Mr Percy Noakes would not act fairly, impartially, or honourably; but he begged it to be distinctly understood, that he said this without the slightest personal disrespect. Mr Hardy defended his honourable friend, in a voice rendered partially unintelligible by emotion and brandy-and-water. The proposition was put to the vote, and there appearing to be only one dissentient voice, Mr Percy Noakes was declared duly elected, and took the chair accordingly.

The business of the meeting now proceeded with great rapidity. The chairman delivered in his estimate of the probable expense of the excursion, and every one present subscribed his proportion thereof. The question was put that 'The Endeavour' be hired for the occasion; Mr Alexander Briggs moved as an amendment, that the word 'Fly' be substituted for the word 'Endeavour;' but after some debate consented to withdraw his opposition. The important ceremony of balloting then commenced. A tea-caddy was placed on a table in a dark corner of the apartment, and every one was provided with two backgammon men; one black and one white.

The chairman with great solemnity then read the following list of the guests whom he proposed to introduce: – Mrs Taunton and two daughters, Mr Wizzle, Mr Simson. The names were respectively balloted for, and Mrs Taunton and her daughters were declared to be black-balled. Mr Percy Noakes and Mr Hardy exchanged glances.

'Is your list prepared, Mr Briggs?' inquired the chairman.

'It is,' replied Alexander, delivering in the following: – 'Mrs Briggs and three daughters, Mr Samuel Briggs.' The previous ceremony was repeated, and Mrs Briggs and three daughters were declared to be black-balled. Mr Alexander Briggs looked rather foolish, and the remainder of the company appeared somewhat overawed by the mysterious nature of the proceedings.

The balloting proceeded; but one little circumstance which Mr Percy Noakes had not originally foreseen, prevented the system working quite as well as he had anticipated – every body was black-balled. Mr Alexander Briggs, by way of retaliation, exercised his power of exclusion in every instance, and the result was, that after three hours had been consumed in incessant balloting, the names of only three gentlemen were found to have been agreed to. In this dilemma what was to be done? either the whole plan must fall to the ground, or a compromise must be effected. The latter alternative was preferable; and Mr

Percy Noakes therefore proposed that the form of balloting should be dispensed with, and that every gentleman should merely be required to state whom he intended to bring. The proposal was readily acceded to; the Tauntons and the Briggses were reinstated, and the party was formed.

The next Wednesday was fixed for the eventful day, and it was unanimously resolved that every member of the committee should wear a piece of blue sarsenet ribbon round his left arm. It appeared from the statement of Mr Percy Noakes, that the boat belonged to the General Steam Navigation Company, and was then lying off the Custom-house; and as he proposed that the dinner and wines should be provided by an eminent city purveyor, it was arranged that Mr Percy Noakes should be on board by seven o'clock to superintend the arrangements, and that the remaining members of the committee, together with the company generally, should be expected to join her by nine o'clock. More brandy-and-water was despatched; several speeches were made by the different law students present; thanks were voted to the chairman, and the meeting separated.

The weather had been beautiful up to this period, and beautiful it continued to be. Sunday passed over, and Mr Percy Noakes became unusually fidgety – rushing constantly to and from the Steam Packet Wharf, to the astonishment of the clerks, and the great emolument of the Holborn cabmen. Tuesday arrived, and the anxiety of Mr Percy Noakes knew no bounds: he was every instant running to the window to look out for clouds; and Mr Hardy astonished the whole square by practising a new comic song for the occasion, in the chairman's chambers.

Uneasy were the slumbers of Mr Percy Noakes that night: he tossed and tumbled about, and had confused dreams of steamers starting off, and gigantic clocks with the hands pointing to a quarter past nine, and the ugly face of Mr Alexander Briggs looking over the boat's side, and grinning as if in derision of his fruitless attempts to move. He made a violent effort to get on board, and awoke. The bright sun was shining cheerfully into the bedroom, and Mr Percy Noakes started up for his watch, in the dreadful expectation of finding his worst dreams realized.

It was just five o'clock. He calculated the time – he should be a good half-hour dressing himself; and as it was a lovely morning, and the tide would be then running down, he would walk leisurely to Strand-lane, and have a boat to the Custom-house.

He dressed himself, took a hasty apology for a breakfast, and sallied forth. The streets looked as lonely and deserted as if they had been crowded overnight for the last time. Here and there an early apprentice, with quenched-looking sleepy eyes, was taking down the shutters of a shop; and a policeman or milk-woman might occasionally be seen pacing slowly along; the servants had not yet begun to clean the doors, or light the fires, and London looked the picture of desolation. At the corner of a bye-street, near Temple-bar, was stationed a 'street breakfast.' The coffee was boiling over a charcoal fire, and large slices of bread and butter were piled one upon the other, like deals in a timber-yard. The company were seated on a form, which, with a view both to security and comfort, was placed against a neighbouring wall. Two young men, whose uproarious mirth and disordered dress bespoke the conviviality of the preceding evening, were treating three 'ladies' and an Irish labourer. A little sweep was standing at a short distance, casting a longing eye at the tempting delicacies; and a policeman was watching the group from the opposite side of the street. The wan looks, and gaudy finery of the wretched thinly-clad females, contrasted as strangely with the gay sun-light, as did their forced merriment with the boisterous hilarity of the two young men, who now and then varied their amusements by 'bonneting' the proprietor of this itinerant coffee-house.

Mr Percy Noakes walked briskly by, and when he turned down Strand-lane, and caught a glimpse of the glistening water, he thought he had never felt so important or so happy in his life.

'Boat, sir!' cried one of the three watermen who were mopping out their boats, and all whistling different tunes. 'Boat, sir!'

'No,' replied Mr Percy Noakes, rather sharply; for the inquiry was not made in a manner at all suitable to his dignity.

'Would you prefer a wessel, sir?' inquired another, to the infinite delight of the 'Jack-in-the-water.'

Mr Percy Noakes replied with a look of the most supreme contempt.

'Did you want to be put on board a steamer, sir?' inquired an old fireman-waterman, very confidentially. He was dressed in a faded red suit, just the colour of the cover of a very old Court-guide.

'Yes, make haste – the Endeavour – off the Custom-house.'

'Endeavour!' cried the man who had convulsed the 'Jack' before. 'Vy, I see the Endeavour go up half an hour ago.'

'So did I,' said another; 'and I should think she'd gone down by this time, for she's a precious sight too full of ladies and gen'lmen.'

Mr Percy Noakes affected to disregard these representations, and stepped into the boat, which the old man, by dint of scrambling, and shoving, and grating, had brought up to the causeway. 'Shove her off,' cried Mr Percy Noakes, and away the boat glided down the river, Mr Percy Noakes seated on the recently mopped seat, and the watermen at the stairs offering to bet him any reasonable sum that he'd never reach the 'Custum-us.'

'Here she is, by Jove!' said the delighted Percy, as they ran alongside the Endeavour.

'Hold hard!' cried the steward over the side, and Mr Percy Noakes jumped on board.

'Hope you'll find every thing as you wished, sir. She looks uncommon well this morning.'

'She does, indeed,' replied the manager, in a state of ecstasy which it is impossible to describe. The deck was scrubbed, and the seats were scrubbed, and there was a bench for the band, and a place for dancing, and a pile of camp-stools, and an awning; and then Mr Percy Noakes bustled down below, and there were the pastrycook's men, and the steward's wife laying out the dinner on two tables the whole length of the cabin; and then Mr Percy Noakes took off his coat, and rushed backwards and forwards, doing nothing, but quite convinced he was assisting every body; and the steward's wife laughed till she cried, and Mr Percy Noakes panted with the violence of his exertions. And then the bell at London-bridge wharf rang, and a Margate boat was just starting, and a Gravesend boat was just starting, and people shouted, and porters ran down the steps with luggage that would crush any men but porters; and sloping boards, with bits of wood nailed on them, were placed between the outside boat and the inside boat, and the passengers ran along them, and looked like so many fowls coming out of an area; and then the bell ceased, and the boards were taken away, and the boats started; and the whole scene was one of the most delightful bustle and confusion that can be imagined.

The time wore on; half-past eight o'clock arrived; the pastry-cook's men went ashore; the dinner was completely laid out, and Mr Percy Noakes locked the principal cabin, and put the key into his pocket, in order that it might be suddenly disclosed in all its magnificence to the eyes of the astonished company. The band came on board, and so did the wine.

Ten minutes to nine, and the committee embarked in a body. There was Mr Hardy in a blue jacket and waistcoat, white trousers, silk stockings, and pumps; habited in full aquatic costume, with a straw hat on his head, and an immense telescope under his arm; and there was the young gentleman with the green spectacles, in nankeen inexplicables, with a ditto waistcoat and bright buttons, like the pictures of Paul – not the saint, but he of Virginia notoriety. The remainder of the committee, dressed in white hats, light jackets, waistcoats, and trousers, looked something between waiters and West India planters.

Nine o'clock struck, and the company arrived in shoals. Mr Samuel Briggs, Mrs Briggs, and the Misses Briggs made their appearance in a smart private wherry. The three guitars, in their respective dark green cases, were carefully stowed away in the bottom of the boat, accompanied by two immense portfolios of music, which it would take at least a week's incessant playing to get through. The Tauntons arrived at the same moment with more music, and a lion – a gentleman with a bass voice and an incipient red moustache. The colours of the Taunton party were pink; those of the Briggses a light blue. The Tauntons had artificial flowers in their bonnets; here the Briggses gained a decided advantage – they wore feathers.

'How d'ye do, dear?' said the Misses Briggs to the Misses Taunton. (The word 'dear' among girls is frequently synonymous with 'wretch.')

'Quite well, thank you, dear,' replied the Misses Taunton to the Misses Briggs; and then there was such a kissing, and congratulating, and shaking of hands, as would induce one to suppose that the two families were the best friends in the world, instead of each wishing the other overboard, as they most sincerely did.

Mr Percy Noakes received the visiters, and bowed to the strange gentleman, as if he should like to know who he was. This was just what Mrs Taunton wanted. Here was an opportunity to astonish the Briggses.

'Oh! I beg your pardon,' said the general of the Taunton party, with a careless air. – 'Captain Helves – Mr Percy Noakes – Mrs Briggs – Captain Helves.'

Mr Percy Noakes bowed very low; the gallant captain did the same with all due ferocity, and the Briggses were clearly overcome.

'Our friend, Mr Wizzle, being unfortunately prevented from coming,' resumed Mrs Taunton, 'I did myself the pleasure of bringing the captain, whose musical talents I knew would be a great acquisition.'

'In the name of the committee I have to thank you for

doing so, and to offer you a most sincere welcome, sir,' replied Percy. (Here the scraping was renewed.) 'But pray be seated – won't you walk aft? Captain, will you conduct Miss Taunton? – Miss Briggs, will you allow me?'

'Where could they have picked up that military man?' inquired Mrs Briggs of Miss Kate Briggs, as they followed the little party.

'I can't imagine,' replied Miss Kate, bursting with vexation; for the very fierce air with which the gallant captain regarded the company, had impressed her with a high sense of his importance.

Boat after boat came alongside, and guest after guest arrived. The invites had been excellently arranged, Mr Percy Noakes having considered it as important that the number of young men should exactly tally with that of the young ladies, as that the quantity of knives on board should be in precise proportion to the forks.

'Now, is every one on board?' inquired Mr Percy Noakes. The committee (who, with their bits of blue ribbon, looked as if they were all going to be bled) bustled about to ascertain the fact, and reported that they might safely start.

'Go on,' cried the master of the boat from the top of one of the paddle-boxes.

'Go on,' echoed the boy, who was stationed over the hatchway to pass the directions down to the engineer; and away went the vessel with that agreeable noise which is peculiar to steamers, and which is composed of a pleasant mixture of creaking, gushing, clanging, and snorting.

'Hoi–oi–oi–oi–oi–oi–o–i–i–i!' shouted half-a-dozen voices from a boat about a quarter of a mile astern.

41

'Ease her!' cried the captain: 'do these people belong to us, sir?'

'Noakes,' exclaimed Hardy, who had been looking at every object, far and near, through the large telescope, 'it's the Fleetwoods and the Wakefields – and two children with them, by Jove!'

'What a shame to bring children!' said every body; 'how very inconsiderate!'

'I say, it would be a good joke to pretend not to see 'em, wouldn't it?' suggested Hardy, to the immense delight of the company generally. A council of war was hastily held, and it was resolved that the new comers should be taken on board, on Mr Hardy's solemnly pledging himself to tease the children during the whole of the day.

'Stop her!' cried the captain.

'Stop her!' repeated the boy; whizz went the steam, and all the young ladies, as in duty bound, screamed in concert. They were only appeased by the assurance of the martial Helves, that the escape of steam consequent on stopping a vessel was seldom attended with any great loss of human life.

Two men ran to the side, and after a good deal of shouting, and swearing, and angling for the wherry with a boat-hook, Mr Fleetwood, and Mrs Fleetwood, and Master Fleetwood, and Mr Wakefield, and Mrs Wakefield, and Miss Wakefield, were safely deposited on the deck. The girl was about six years old, the boy about four; the former was dressed in a white frock with a pink sash and a dog's-eared-looking little spencer, a straw bonnet and green veil, six inches by three and a half: the latter was attired for the occasion in a nankeen frock, between the bottom of which and the top of his plaid socks a considerable portion of two small mottled legs was discernible. He had a light blue cap with a gold band and tassel on his head, and a damp piece of gingerbread in his hand, with which he had slightly embossed his dear little countenance.

The boat once more started off; the band played 'Off she goes;' the major part of the company conversed cheerfully in groups, and the old gentlemen walked up and down the deck in pairs, as perseveringly and gravely as if they were doing a match against time for an immense stake. They ran briskly down the Pool; the gentlemen pointed out the Docks, the Thames Police-office, and other elegant public edifices; and the young ladies exhibited a proper display of horror and bashfulness at the appearance of the coal-whippers and ballast-heavers. Mr Hardy told stories to the married ladies, at which they laughed very much in their pocket-handkerchiefs, and hit him on the knuckles with their fans, declaring him to be 'a naughty man – a shocking creature' – and so forth; and Captain Helves gave slight descriptions of battles and duels, with a most bloodthirsty air, which made him the admiration of the women, and the envy of the men. Quadrilling commenced; Captain Helves danced one set with Miss Emily Taunton, and another set with Miss Sophia Taunton. Mrs Taunton was in ecstasies. The victory appeared to be complete; but, alas! the inconstancy of man! Having performed this necessary duty, he attached himself solely to Miss Julia Briggs, with whom he danced no less than three sets consecutively, and from whose side he evinced no intention of stirring for the remainder of the day.

Mr Hardy having played one or two very brilliant fantasias on the Jews'-harp, and having frequently repeated the exquisitely amusing joke of slily chalking a large cross on the back of some member of the committee, Mr Percy Noakes expressed his hope that some of their musical friends would oblige the company by a display of their abilities.

'Perhaps,' he said in a very insinuating manner, 'Captain Helves will oblige us.' Mrs Taunton's countenance lighted up, for the captain only sang duets, and couldn't sing them with any body but one of her daughters.

'Really,' said that warlike individual, 'I should be very happy, but –'

'Oh! pray do,' cried all the young ladies.

'Miss Sophia, have you any objection to join in a duet?'

'Oh! not the slightest,' returned the young lady, in a tone which clearly showed she had the greatest possible objection.

'Shall I accompany you, dear?' inquired one of the Miss Briggses, with the bland intention of spoiling the effect.

'Very much obliged to you, Miss Briggs,' sharply retorted Mrs Taunton, who saw through the manœuvre; 'my daughters always sing without accompaniments.'

'And without voices,' tittered Mrs Briggs, in a low tone.

'Perhaps,' said Mrs Taunton, reddening, for she guessed the tenor of the observation, though she had not heard it clearly – 'Perhaps it would be as well for some people, if their voices were not quite so audible as they are to other people.'

'And perhaps, if gentlemen, who are kidnapped to pay attention to some persons' daughters, had not sufficient discernment to pay attention to other persons' daughters,' returned Mrs Briggs, 'some persons would not be so ready to display that ill-temper, which, thank God, distinguishes them from other persons.'

'Persons!' ejaculated Mrs Taunton.

'Yes; persons, ma'am,' replied Mrs Briggs.

'Insolence!'

'Creature!'

'Hush! hush!' interrupted Mr Percy Noakes, who was one of the very few by whom this dialogue had been overheard. 'Hush! – pray silence for the duet.'

After a great deal of preparatory crowing and humming, the captain began the following duet from the opera of 'Paul and Virginia,' in that grunting tone in which a man gets down, Heaven knows where, without the remotest chance of ever getting up again. This, in private circles, is frequently designated 'a bass voice.'

> 'See (sung the captain) from o–ce–an ri–sing
> Bright flames the or–b of d–ay.
> From yon gro–ve, the varied so–ngs —'

Here the singer was interrupted by varied cries of the most dreadful description, proceeding from some grove in the immediate vicinity of the starboard paddle-box.

'My child!' screamed Mrs Fleetwood. 'My child! it is his voice – I know it.'

Mr Fleetwood, accompanied by several gentlemen, here rushed to the quarter from whence the noise proceeded, and an exclamation of horror burst from the company; the general impression being, that the little innocent had either got his head in the water, or his legs in the machinery.

'What is the matter?' shouted the agonized father, as he returned with the child in his arms.

'Oh! oh! oh!' screamed the small sufferer again.

'What is the matter, dear?' inquired the father once more – hastily stripping off the nankeen frock, for the purpose of ascertaining whether the child had one bone which was not smashed to pieces.

'Oh! oh! – I'm so frightened.'

'What at, dear? – what at?' said the mother, soothing the sweet infant.

'Oh! he's been making such dreadful faces at me,' cried the boy, relapsing into convulsions at the bare recollection.

'He! – who?' cried every body, crowding round him.

'Oh! – him,' replied the child, pointing at Hardy, who affected to be the most concerned of the whole group.

The real state of the case at once flashed upon the minds of all present, with the exception of the Fleetwoods and the Wakefields. The facetious Hardy, in fulfilment of his promise, had watched the child to a remote part of the vessel, and, suddenly appearing before him with the most awful contortions of visage, had produced his paroxysm of terror. Of course, he now observed that it was hardly necessary for him to deny the accusation; and the unfortunate little victim was accordingly led below, after receiving sundry thumps on the head from both his parents, for having the wickedness to tell a story.

This little interruption having been adjusted, the captain resumed and Miss Emily chimed in, in due course. The duet was loudly applauded, and, certainly, the perfect independence of the parties deserved great commendation. Miss Emily sung her part without the slightest reference to the captain, and the captain sang so loud that he had not the slightest idea of what was being done by his partner. After having gone through the last few eighteen or nineteen bars by himself, therefore, he acknowledged the plaudits of the circle with that air of self-denial which men always assume when they think they have done something to astonish the company, though they don't exactly know what.

'Now,' said Mr Percy Noakes, who had just ascended from the fore-cabin, where he had been busily engaged in decanting the wine, 'if the Misses Briggs will oblige us with something before dinner, I am sure we shall be very much delighted.'

One of those hums of admiration followed the suggestion, which one frequently hears in society, when nobody has the most distant notion of what he is expressing his approval of. The three Misses Briggs looked modestly at their mamma, and the mamma looked approvingly at her daughters, and Mrs Taunton looked scornfully at all of them. The Misses Briggs asked for their guitars, and several gentlemen seriously damaged the cases in their anxiety to present them. Then there was a very interesting production of three little keys for the aforesaid cases, and a melodramatic expression of horror at finding a string broken; and a vast deal of screwing and tightening, and winding and tuning, during which Mrs Briggs expatiated to those near her on the immense difficulty of playing a guitar, and hinted at the wondrous proficiency of her daughters in that mystic art. Mrs Taunton whispered to a neighbour that it was 'quite sickening!' and the Misses Taunton tried to look as if they knew how to play, but disdained to do so.

At length the Misses Briggs began in real earnest. It was a new Spanish composition, for three voices and three guitars. The effect was electrical. All eyes were turned upon the captain, who was reported to have once passed through Spain with his regiment, and who, of course, must be well acquainted with the national music. He was in raptures. This was sufficient; the trio was encored – the applause was universal, and never had the Tauntons suffered such a complete defeat.

'Bravo! bravo!' ejaculated the captain; – 'Bravo!'

'Pretty! isn't it, sir?' inquired Mr Samuel Briggs, with the air of a self-satisfied showman. By the by, these were the first words he had been heard to utter since he left Boswell-court the evening before.

'De–lightful!' returned the captain, with a flourish, and a military cough; – 'de–lightful!'

'Sweet instrument!' said an old gentleman with a bald head, who had been trying all the morning to look through a telescope, inside the glass of which Mr Hardy had fixed a large black wafer.

'Did you ever hear a Portuguese tambarine?' inquired that jocular individual.

'Did *you* ever hear a tom-tom, sir?' sternly inquired the captain, who lost no opportunity of showing off his travels, real or pretended.

'A what?' asked Hardy, rather taken aback.

'A tom-tom.'

'Never!'

'Nor a gum-gum?'

'Never!'

'What *is* a gum-gum?' eagerly inquired several young ladies.

'When I was in the East Indies,' replied the captain, (here was a discovery – he had been in the East Indies!) – 'when I was in the East Indies, I was once stopping a few thousand miles up the country, on a visit at the house of a very particular friend of mine, Ram Chowdar Doss Azuph Al Bowlar – a devilish pleasant fellow. As we were enjoying our hookahs one evening in the cool verandah in front of his villa, we were rather surprised by the sudden appearance of thirty-four of his Kit-ma-gars (for he had rather a large establishment there), accompanied by an equal number of Consumars, approaching the house with a threatening aspect, and beating a tom-tom. The Ram started up —'

'The who?' inquired the bald gentleman, intensely interested.

'The Ram – Ram Chowdar –'

'Oh!' said the old gentleman, 'I beg your pardon; it really didn't occur to me; pray go on.'

'– Started up and drew a pistol. "Helves," said he, "my boy," – he always called me, my boy – "Helves," said he, "do you hear that tom-tom?" – "I do," said I. His countenance, which before was pale, assumed a most frightful appearance; his whole visage was distorted, and his frame shaken by violent emotions. "Do you see that gum-gum?" said he. "No," said I, staring about me. "You don't?" said he. "No, I'll be damned if I do", said I; "and what's more, I don't know what a gum-gum is," said I. I really thought the man would have dropped. He drew me aside, and, with an expression of agony I shall never forget, said in a low whisper —'

'Dinner's on the table, ladies,' interrupted the steward's wife.

'Will you allow me?' said the captain, immediately suiting the action to the word, and escorting Miss Julia Briggs to the cabin, with as much ease as if he had finished the story.

'What an extraordinary circumstance!' ejaculated the same old gentleman, preserving his listening attitude.

'What a traveller!' said the young ladies.

'What a singular name!' exclaimed the gentlemen, rather confused by the coolness of the whole affair.

'I wish he had finished the story,' said an old lady. 'I wonder what a gum-gum really is?'

'By Jove!' exclaimed Hardy, who until now had been lost in utter amazement, 'I don't know what it may be in India, but in England I think a gum-gum has very much the same meaning as a humbug.'

'How illiberal! how envious!' said every body, as they made for the cabin, fully impressed with a belief in the captain's amazing adventures. Helves was the sole lion for the remainder of the day – impudence and the marvellous are sure passports to any society.

The party had by this time reached their destination, and put about on their return home. The wind, which had been with them the whole day, was now directly in their teeth; the weather had become gradually more and more overcast; and the sky, water, and shore, were all of that dull, heavy, uniform lead-colour, which house-painters daub in the first instance over a street-door which is gradually approaching a state of convalescence. It had been 'spitting' with rain for the last half-hour, and now began to pour in good earnest. The wind was freshening very fast, and the waterman at the wheel had unequivocally expressed his opinion that there would shortly be a squall. A slight motion on the part of the vessel now and then, seemed to suggest the possibility of its pitching to a very uncomfortable extent in the event of its blowing harder; and every timber began to creak as if the boat were an overladen clothes-basket. Sea-sickness, however, is like a belief in ghosts – every one entertains some misgivings on the subject, but few will acknowledge them. The majority of the company, therefore, endeavoured to look peculiarly happy, feeling all the while especially miserable.

'Don't it rain?' inquired the old gentleman before noticed, when, by dint of squeezing and jamming, they were all seated at table.

'I think it does – a little,' replied Mr Percy Noakes, who could hardly hear himself speak, in consequence of the pattering on the deck.

'Don't it blow?' inquired some one else.

'No – I don't think it does,' responded Hardy, sincerely wishing that he could persuade himself it did not, for he sat near the door, and was almost blown off his seat.

'It'll soon clear up,' said Mr Percy Noakes, in a cheerful tone.

'Oh, certainly!' ejaculated the committee generally.

'No doubt of it,' said the remainder of the company, whose attention was now pretty well engrossed by the serious business of eating, carving, taking wine, and so forth.

The throbbing motion of the engine was but too perceptible. There was a large, substantial cold boiled leg of mutton at the bottom of the table, shaking like blanc-mange; a hearty sirloin of beef looked as if it had been suddenly seized with the palsy; and some tongues, which were placed on dishes rather too large for them, were going through the most surprising evolutions, darting from side to side, and from end to end, like a fly in an inverted wine-glass. Then the sweets shook and trembled till it was quite impossible to help them, and people gave up the attempt in despair; and the pigeon-pies looked as if the birds, whose legs were

51

stuck outside, were trying to get them in. The table vibrated and started like a feverish pulse, and the very legs were slightly convulsed – every thing was shaking and jarring. The beams in the roof of the cabin seemed as if they were put there for the sole purpose of giving people headaches, and several elderly gentlemen became ill-tempered in consequence. As fast as the steward put the fire-irons up, they *would* fall down again; and the more the ladies and gentlemen tried to sit comfortably on their seats, the more the seats seemed to slide away from the ladies and gentlemen. Several ominous demands were made for small glasses of brandy; the countenances of the company gradually underwent the most extraordinary changes; and one gentleman was observed suddenly to rush from table without the slightest ostensible reason, and dart up the steps with incredible swiftness, thereby greatly damaging both himself and the steward, who happened to be coming down at the same moment.

The cloth was removed; the dessert was laid on the table, and the glasses were filled. The motion of the boat increased; several members of the party began to feel rather vague and misty, and looked as if they had only just got up. The young gentleman with the spectacles, who had been in a fluctuating state for some time – one moment bright, and another dismal, like a revolving light on the sea-coast – rashly announced his wish to propose a toast. After several ineffectual attempts to preserve his perpendicular, the young gentleman, having managed to hook himself to the centre leg of the table with his left hand, proceeded as follows:

'Ladies and gentlemen. – A gentleman is among us – I may say a stranger – (here some painful thought seemed to strike the orator; he paused, and looked extremely odd) whose talents, whose travels, whose cheerfulness –'

'I beg your pardon, Edkins,' hastily interrupted Mr Percy Noakes. – 'Hardy, what's the matter?'

'Nothing,' replied the 'funny gentleman', who had just life enough left to utter two consecutive syllables.

'Will you have some brandy?'

'No,' replied Hardy, in a tone of great indignation, and looking about as comfortable as Temple-bar in a Scotch mist; 'what should I want brandy for?'

'Will you go on deck?'

'No, I will not.' This was said with a most determined air, and in a voice which might have been taken for an imitation of any thing; it was quite as much like a guinea-pig as a bassoon.

'I beg your pardon, Edkins,' said the courteous Percy; 'I thought our friend was ill. Pray go on.'

A pause.

'Pray go on.'

'Mr Edkins *is* gone,' cried somebody.

'I beg your pardon, sir,' said the steward, running up to Mr Percy Noakes, 'I beg your pardon, sir, but the gentleman as just went on deck – him with the green spectacles – is uncommon bad, to be sure; and the young man as played the wiolin says, that unless he has some brandy he can't answer for the consequences. He says he has a wife and two children, whose werry subsistence depends on his breaking a wessel, and that he expects to do so every moment. The flageolet's been very ill, but he's better, only he's in such a dreadful prusperation.'

All disguise was now useless; the company staggered on deck, the gentlemen tried to see nothing but the clouds, and

53

the ladies, muffled up in such shawls and cloaks as they had brought with them, lay about on the seats and under the seats, in the most wretched condition. Never was such a blowing, and raining, and pitching, and tossing, endured by any pleasure party before. Several remonstrances were sent down below on the subject of Master Fleetwood, but they were totally unheeded in consequence of the indisposition of his natural protectors. That interesting child screamed at the very top of his voice, until he had no voice left to scream with, and then Miss Wakefield began, and screamed for the remainder of the passage.

Mr Hardy was observed some hours afterwards in an attitude which induced his friends to suppose that he was busily engaged in contemplating the beauties of the deep; they only regretted that his taste for the picturesque should lead him to remain so long in a position, very injurious at all times, but especially so to an individual labouring under a tendency of blood to the head.

The party arrived off the Custom-house at about two o'clock on the Thursday morning – dispirited and worn out. The Tauntons were too ill to quarrel with the Briggses, and the Briggses were too wretched to annoy the Tauntons. One of the guitar-cases was lost on its passage to a hackney-coach, and Mrs Briggs has not scrupled to state that the Tauntons bribed a porter to throw it down an area. Mr Alexander Briggs opposes vote by ballot – he says from personal experience of its inefficacy; and Mr Samuel Briggs, whenever he is asked to express his sentiments on the point, says that he has no opinion on that or any other subject.

Mr Edkins – the young gentleman in the green

spectacles – makes a speech on every occasion on which a speech can possibly be made, the eloquence of which can only be equalled by its length. In the event of his not being previously appointed to a judgeship, it is most probable that he will practise as a barrister in the New Central Criminal Court.

Captain Helves continued his attention to Miss Julia Briggs, whom he might possibly have espoused, if it had not unfortunately happened that Mr Samuel arrested him in the way of business, pursuant to instructions received from Messrs Scroggins and Payne, whose town debts the gallant captain had condescended to collect, but whose accounts, with the indiscretion so peculiar to military minds, he had omitted to keep with that dull accuracy which custom has rendered necessary. Mrs Taunton complains that she has been much deceived in him. He introduced himself to the family on board a Gravesend steam-packet, and certainly, therefore, ought to have proved respectable.

Mr Percy Noakes is as light-hearted and careless as ever. We have described him as a general favourite in his private circle, and trust he may find a kindly-disposed friend or two in public.

1. BOCCACCIO · *Mrs Rosie and the Priest*
2. GERARD MANLEY HOPKINS · *As kingfishers catch fire*
3. *The Saga of Gunnlaug Serpent-tongue*
4. THOMAS DE QUINCEY · *On Murder Considered as One of the Fine Arts*
5. FRIEDRICH NIETZSCHE · *Aphorisms on Love and Hate*
6. JOHN RUSKIN · *Traffic*
7. PU SONGLING · *Wailing Ghosts*
8. JONATHAN SWIFT · *A Modest Proposal*
9. *Three Tang Dynasty Poets*
10. WALT WHITMAN · *On the Beach at Night Alone*
11. KENKŌ · *A Cup of Sake Beneath the Cherry Trees*
12. BALTASAR GRACIÁN · *How to Use Your Enemies*
13. JOHN KEATS · *The Eve of St Agnes*
14. THOMAS HARDY · *Woman much missed*
15. GUY DE MAUPASSANT · *Femme Fatale*
16. MARCO POLO · *Travels in the Land of Serpents and Pearls*
17. SUETONIUS · *Caligula*
18. APOLLONIUS OF RHODES · *Jason and Medea*
19. ROBERT LOUIS STEVENSON · *Olalla*
20. KARL MARX AND FRIEDRICH ENGELS · *The Communist Manifesto*
21. PETRONIUS · *Trimalchio's Feast*
22. JOHANN PETER HEBEL · *How a Ghastly Story Was Brought to Light by a Common or Garden Butcher's Dog*
23. HANS CHRISTIAN ANDERSEN · *The Tinder Box*
24. RUDYARD KIPLING · *The Gate of the Hundred Sorrows*
25. DANTE · *Circles of Hell*
26. HENRY MAYHEW · *Of Street Piemen*
27. HAFEZ · *The nightingales are drunk*
28. GEOFFREY CHAUCER · *The Wife of Bath*
29. MICHEL DE MONTAIGNE · *How We Weep and Laugh at the Same Thing*
30. THOMAS NASHE · *The Terrors of the Night*
31. EDGAR ALLAN POE · *The Tell-Tale Heart*
32. MARY KINGSLEY · *A Hippo Banquet*
33. JANE AUSTEN · *The Beautifull Cassandra*
34. ANTON CHEKHOV · *Gooseberries*
35. SAMUEL TAYLOR COLERIDGE · *Well, they are gone, and here must I remain*
36. JOHANN WOLFGANG VON GOETHE · *Sketchy, Doubtful, Incomplete Jottings*
37. CHARLES DICKENS · *The Great Winglebury Duel*
38. HERMAN MELVILLE · *The Maldive Shark*
39. ELIZABETH GASKELL · *The Old Nurse's Story*
40. NIKOLAY LESKOV · *The Steel Flea*

41. HONORÉ DE BALZAC · *The Atheist's Mass*
42. CHARLOTTE PERKINS GILMAN · *The Yellow Wall-Paper*
43. C.P. CAVAFY · *Remember, Body . . .*
44. FYODOR DOSTOEVSKY · *The Meek One*
45. GUSTAVE FLAUBERT · *A Simple Heart*
46. NIKOLAI GOGOL · *The Nose*
47. SAMUEL PEPYS · *The Great Fire of London*
48. EDITH WHARTON · *The Reckoning*
49. HENRY JAMES · *The Figure in the Carpet*
50. WILFRED OWEN · *Anthem For Doomed Youth*
51. WOLFGANG AMADEUS MOZART · *My Dearest Father*
52. PLATO · *Socrates' Defence*
53. CHRISTINA ROSSETTI · *Goblin Market*
54. *Sindbad the Sailor*
55. SOPHOCLES · *Antigone*
56. RYŪNOSUKE AKUTAGAWA · *The Life of a Stupid Man*
57. LEO TOLSTOY · *How Much Land Does A Man Need?*
58. GIORGIO VASARI · *Leonardo da Vinci*
59. OSCAR WILDE · *Lord Arthur Savile's Crime*
60. SHEN FU · *The Old Man of the Moon*
61. AESOP · *The Dolphins, the Whales and the Gudgeon*
62. MATSUO BASHŌ · *Lips too Chilled*
63. EMILY BRONTË · *The Night is Darkening Round Me*
64. JOSEPH CONRAD · *To-morrow*
65. RICHARD HAKLUYT · *The Voyage of Sir Francis Drake Around the Whole Globe*
66. KATE CHOPIN · *A Pair of Silk Stockings*
67. CHARLES DARWIN · *It was snowing butterflies*
68. BROTHERS GRIMM · *The Robber Bridegroom*
69. CATULLUS · *I Hate and I Love*
70. HOMER · *Circe and the Cyclops*
71. D. H. LAWRENCE · *Il Duro*
72. KATHERINE MANSFIELD · *Miss Brill*
73. OVID · *The Fall of Icarus*
74. SAPPHO · *Come Close*
75. IVAN TURGENEV · *Kasyan from the Beautiful Lands*
76. VIRGIL · *O Cruel Alexis*
77. H. G. WELLS · *A Slip under the Microscope*
78. HERODOTUS · *The Madness of Cambyses*
79. *Speaking of Siva*
80. *The Dhammapada*